™

Special thanks to
Emily Sharratt

Reading Consultant: Prue Goodwin, lecturer in literacy and children's books.

ORCHARD BOOKS

First published in 2020 by The Watts Publishing Group

3 5 7 9 10 8 6 4

©2020 Pokémon. ©1997-2017 Nintendo, Creatures,
GAME FREAK, TV Tokyo, ShoPro, JR Kikaku. TM, ® Nintendo.

Text has been adapted from TV episodes, speech may not match exactly final audio

A CIP catalogue record for this book is available from the British Library.

ISBN 978 1 40835 746 0

Printed and bound in China

The paper and board used in this book are made from wood from responsible sources.

Orchard Books
An imprint of Hachette Children's Group
Part of The Watts Publishing Group Limited
Carmelite House, 50 Victoria Embankment, London EC4Y 0DZ

An Hachette UK Company
www.hachette.co.uk
www.hachettechildrens.co.uk

LEGENDARY
ULTRA BEASTS

ORCHARD

MEET ASH AND PIKACHU!

ASH

A Pokémon dreamer who wants to have it all – including becoming a Pokémon Master!

PIKACHU

Ash's first partner Pokémon and long-time companion!

LOOK OUT FOR THESE POKÉMON

COSMOG

ROWLET

LUNALA

SOLGALEO

LITTEN

CONTENTS

PART ONE
A New Mystery

CHAPTER ONE

The Sleeping Promise

Ash and Pikachu peered through
the mist at a strange tower. Ash
knew he had to get closer.

When he approached, he saw
a doorway in the tower.

As he stepped nearer, the stair beneath his foot cracked and he only just jumped away in time. Looking around, Ash saw that all the structures around him were old and crumbling.

Two flashes lit up the sky and from them burst two majestic-looking Pokémon.

"Solgaleo! Lunala!" breathed Ash in wonderment.

The two Pokémon came closer and Ash found himself saying, "I understand, Solgaleo! I promise, Lunala!"

Solgaleo and Lunala nodded.
Then they disappeared back
into the sky in another blinding
flash of light.

Ash squinted. He could see
a strange, cloud-like shape.
But before he could work out
what it was, a loud sound rang
through his head.

Rrrrrrrrrrrring!
Rrrrrrrrrring!

"Wake up, Ash! You're going to be late for school!"

"I promise," Ash mumbled sleepily.

The next thing he knew, something was hitting him across his face.

"Huh? Ow!" Ash opened his eyes to see Litten sitting on his chest. Its tail was a blur as it hit his cheeks.

Ash's Rotom Dex was hovering anxiously above.

"It's time to stop dreaming and get ready for school, Ash!"

Ash was living with Professor Kukui while he stayed on Melemele Island in the Alola Region.

CHAPTER TWO

Alola Woman of the Year

Ash fed the Pokémon belonging to him and the Professor and got his own breakfast. But he couldn't get the dream out of his head.

"What did I promise?" he wondered, taking a sip of juice.

"Excuse me!" shouted Rotom Dex, interrupting Ash's thoughts. "My breakfast is information – it's time for the news!"

"The Alola Woman of the Year award has just been announced," the TV news reader informed them. "This year's prize goes to the researcher Professor Burnet."

"Oh, wow!" exclaimed Professor Kukui.

"Do you know her, Professor?" asked Ash.

"I do," replied the Professor. "We're fellow researchers."

The news reader listed all of Professor Burnet's achievements. "What does Professor Burnet research?" asked Rotom Dex.

"Ultra Wormholes," Professor Kukui answered.

"Ultra Wormholes?" Ash repeated, feeling a tingle run down his spine.

"I'll tell you all about them, Ash," said Professor Kukui, "but not now. I need to leave for the Pokémon School, and you should set off soon too!"

A little later, Ash, Pikachu and Rotom Dex were on their way to school. Pikachu suddenly stopped and ran into the woodland.

"Pikachu? Where are you going?" Ash called as he ran after his Pokémon.

Pikachu came to an abrupt stop, making Ash run into the back of it.

"Look, Ash!" whispered Rotom Dex.

Hovering above the bushes was Tapu Koko, the Guardian Pokémon of Melemele Island.

CHAPTER THREE

Unknown Pokémon

Ash had met the Guardian Pokémon Tapu Koko before, when he first arrived on Melemele Island.

As they watched, the bushes Tapu Koko had been hovering over rustled.

"What's that?" Ash wondered aloud, moving closer.

Nestled in the leaves and glowing with a soft light was a Pokémon. Ash had never seen this Pokémon before but its cloud-like shape seemed familiar to him.

Pikachu approached and

nuzzled the new Pokémon's face, making it gurgle.

"It's asleep!" Ash said, gently picking it up. As he did, parts of his dream suddenly came back to him.

"I promise … I promise!"

"What are you talking about, Ash?" asked Rotom Dex.

"This is what I promised in my dream. I would find this Pokémon and take care of it."

"Illogical! Illogical!" declared Rotom Dex, a note of panic in its electronic voice.

"I wonder what kind of Pokémon it is," said Ash, stroking the sleeping creature.

"Leave the data research to me!" said Rotom Dex, happy to be helping again.

But a moment later, its face

was puzzled and its screen blank. "That's strange. My research hasn't found any Pokémon data at all!"

PART TWO
A Busy Day at Pokémon School

CHAPTER FOUR

A New Pokémon

"Alola, class," said Professor Kukui, smiling at his pupils from the Pokémon School.

"Alola, Professor Kukui!" they replied.

"Wait a minute, where's Ash?" the Professor asked.

"He isn't here yet," answered Mallow, one of Ash's new friends.

"That's odd. I'm sure he was going to leave home right after me!"

Just then, Ash came flying into the classroom. "Professor Kukui! Professor Kukui!" he shouted out of breath.

"We've discovered a Pokémon not in my database!" exclaimed Rotom Dex.

"It's the same one from my dream last night!" said Ash. "I promised someone I'd find it and take care of it and … and … and …"

"All right," Professor Kukui said, laughing. "Calm down and take a breath. Now, let's hear more about this Pokémon. Where is it?"

"It's in my bag," said Ash. He unzipped his backpack to reveal the new Pokémon snuggled next to Rowlet.

Ash's classmates and their

Pokémon gathered round.
They all gasped as the
unknown Pokémon floated
up into the air.

"It floats!" Ash exclaimed.

"But it's still asleep!"
Rotom Dex added.

Lillie was looking through a book of Alolan Pokémon. "It doesn't appear at all in here," she said in surprise.

"This could be a brand-new kind of Pokémon!" said Sophocles.

"And that would make Ash the one who discovered it!" said Kiawe.

CHAPTER FIVE

Hush, Little Nebby

"If this is a new Pokémon, we should find out everything we can about it," said Professor Kukui. "And we should name it."

"Nebula … Nebby," murmured Lillie.

"What was that?" Ash asked.

Lillie blushed. "Well, it has stars glittering inside it. And it floats like a cloud. A nebula is a cloud of gas with stars inside. I was thinking we could call it Nebby."

"Like a mini nebula," said Ash. "I like it!"

The others all agreed and Lillie blushed even more.

They all smiled and gazed fondly at Nebby.

Then the little Pokémon
finally decided to wake up and
began to cry at the top of its
voice.

"Oh no," said Ash, swaying
with Nebby in a way he hoped
was soothing. "Don't cry,
Nebby, don't cry."

After several minutes, Nebby's crying only got louder. Ash thrust it at Kiawe. "Your turn!"

But Kiawe's singing didn't calm Nebby either. Finally, it settled in Mallow's arms and they all breathed a sigh of relief.

"Now that Nebby is in a better mood we should try to find out what it likes to eat," said Professor Kukui.

They put out different Pokémon foods, but Nebby wasn't interested in any of them.

Next they tried all their own
food, but that didn't work
either.

Just then, Sophocles took out
a bag of his star candy. Nebby
floated up, a look of interest on
its face.

"Want to try it?" Ash asked.

He held out a star candy and Nebby gobbled it up. And the next one … and the next one!

CHAPTER SIX

Unexpected Visitors

After school, Sophocles took
Ash and Lillie to a supermarket.
They wanted to buy lots of star
candy for Nebby.

This meant that Ash and Lillie arrived home later than Professor Kukui.

As they arrived back at the house, Ash was surprised to see a helicopter outside. Its blades were still turning.

"Hey, Ash," said the Professor. He was at the door as they waved goodbye to Sophocles.

"We have some visitors who would like to meet you."

"Oh?" said Ash.

"They want to meet Nebby too," Professor Kukui went on. "And one of them in particular really wants to see you, Lillie."

"Me?" Lillie said, sounding puzzled.

The Professor nodded and led them into the living room. A woman with long, white-blonde hair dashed forwards and flung her arms around Lillie.

"Lillie!" she exclaimed. "My baby!"

"Mum! I'm not a baby," said Lillie, sounding unusually cross as she smoothed her hair.

"Let me introduce you to everyone," said Professor Kukui hurriedly.

"Lillie's mother's name is Lusamine. She is head of the organisation leading the research that Professor Burnet does." He gestured to the other woman in the room, who Ash recognised from the news

that morning.

"Professor Burnet!" Ash said in surprise.

PART THREE

The Legend of
the Ultra Beasts

CHAPTER SEVEN

An Ancient Alolan Battle

"I'm very pleased to meet you, Ash," said Professor Burnet. "Professor Kukui has told me so much about you."

"Me too, Ash," said Lusamine.

"And now, if you wouldn't mind, we would like to meet Nebby."

"OK," said Ash, putting his backpack onto the floor and carefully lifting Nebby out. He was excited to hear what the famous professor could tell them about his new discovery.

Everyone gathered around. Nebby giggled and wriggled in Ash's arms.

"Isn't it amazing?" said Lusamine.

Professor Burnet nodded.

"As I thought – it seems to be an Ultra Beast." said the Professor.

"What's an Ultra Beast?" Ash asked.

"Let me show you," said Professor Burnet, leading them over to Professor Kukui's computer.

She pulled up images of ancient cave paintings.

"That's Tapu Koko!" Ash exclaimed, recognising one of the painted figures.

"That's right," said Professor Burnet, as the screen showed all sorts of mysterious images. "A long time ago, some strange creatures suddenly appeared in Alola from another world. They challenged the Island Guardians to a terrible battle. Have you ever heard that legend?"

Ash shook his head.

Lillie spoke up. "I have, I've read all about it. These strange creatures were known as Ultra Beasts, weren't they?"

"They were," Professor Burnet agreed.

"And you really believe Nebby could be one of these Ultra Beasts?" Ash asked.

"I do," the Professor replied.

CHAPTER EIGHT

The Altar of the Sunne

"Any physical beings from that other world – including Ultra Beasts – give off a sort of aura," Professor Burnet explained. "Our laboratory monitors these aura."

"Last night we measured a big spike in the readings." She pointed to the screen again where a tower had appeared. "It happened right by the Altar of the Sunne"

"That's it!" said Ash, gazing at the screen.

"What do you mean, Ash?"

"That's the place I saw in my dream!"

The others all looked at Ash in amazement.

"The Altar of Sunne is said to be the site of a dreadful battle."

"It took place between the Island Guardians and the Ultra Beasts," Lusamine said. "Very little is known about this time in history. But our research into Ultra Beasts always leads us back to this place."

"Did you see anything else in your dream?" asked the Professor.

"Yes," said Ash slowly, as more memories came back to him. "Two amazing-looking Pokémon appeared in the sky. They were called Solgaleo and Lunala—"

"Solgaleo?" asked Professor Kukui.

"Lunala?" said Professor Burnet, looking stunned.

"All we know about those Pokémon is what we've learned through legend," said Lusamine. "And now they've appeared to you, Ash."

Ash didn't know what to say.
Could he really have seen the
Pokémon from the legend in
his dream?

CHAPTER NINE

A Promise Kept

"Ash, will you let us look after Nebby at the Aether Foundation, our research centre?" said Lusamine, interrupting Ash's thoughts. "We take great care of all the Pokémon we study there, don't worry."

"The thing is," Ash began, "I promised them in my dream. I promised Solgaleo and Lunala that I would take care of Nebby. I can't break that promise."

"I understand that, Ash," said Lusamine gently, "but taking care of an Ultra Beast is a lot of responsibility. Are you sure—"

"You should know that Ash is a powerful Trainer," Lillie interrupted, staring at her mother.

"Not only that, but he received a Z-Ring and Z-Crystal from Tapu Koko itself!"

"From the Island Guardian of Melemele?" said Professor Burnet, looking impressed.

"It's true," Professor Kukui confirmed.

"Well that settles it then," said Lusamine. "Of course you can ask us for help whenever you need it, Ash and I hope you will. But Solgaleo and Lunala must have had their reasons for entrusting Nebby to your care. And I for one would like to find out what they are!

Nebby can stay with you."

"Hmmm, just what we need in this house," muttered Rotom Dex. "Another oversleeper!"

The End

DON'T MISS THESE OTHER OFFICIAL POKÉMON BOOKS